Bad Chad Wears Plaid

Written by Bridgette P. Hurt

Illustrated by Stacy Hummel

To my sweet and amazing husband, Bryant.
To my sister, Yolanda (Yo) and her dog, Chad. Thank you, Thank you, and Thank you! To my mother, we did it again!
To my father, thank you for your wisdom.
To my niece, Lailah, and my brother Junie- thanks for your support!

A dog named Chad was standing on the couch looking out the window.

Chad wondered where did his owner go?
You see, Chad knew that his owner- Yo, left the house many hours ago!

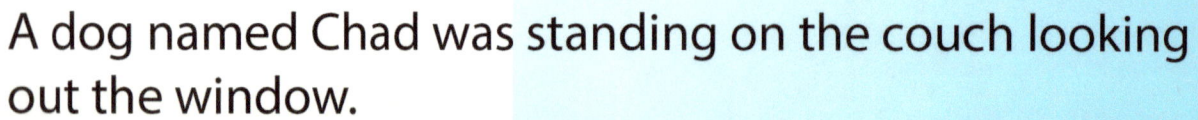

Chad was feeling sad, so he thought of something to make himself glad, so...
he jumped off the couch to look for his Dad.

You see, Chad's dad is named Brad and Brad is more of a grouch.

Brad's favorite thing is lying around the house like a slouch.

Brad

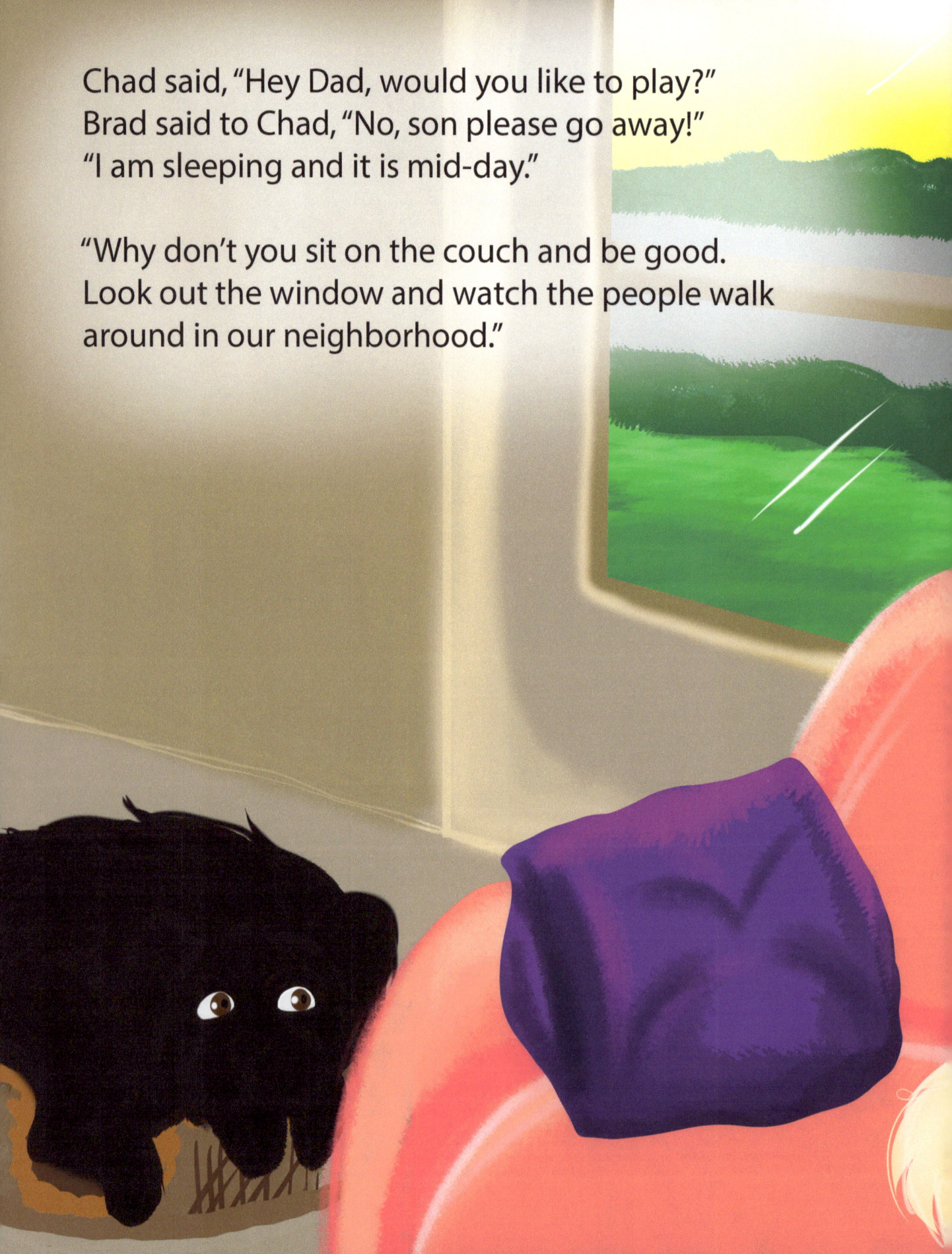

Chad said, "Hey Dad, would you like to play?"
Brad said to Chad, "No, son please go away!"
"I am sleeping and it is mid-day."

"Why don't you sit on the couch and be good.
Look out the window and watch the people walk
around in our neighborhood."

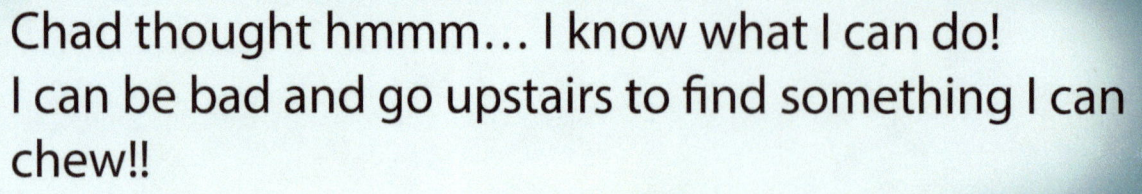

Chad thought hmmm… I know what I can do!
I can be bad and go upstairs to find something I can
chew!!

So Chad went upstairs and looked to see which room he should start.

You see, Yo had four rooms decorated with STRIPES, POLKA DOTS, PLAIDS, AND HEARTS!

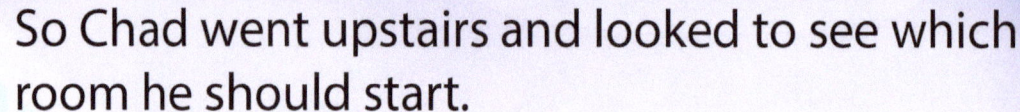

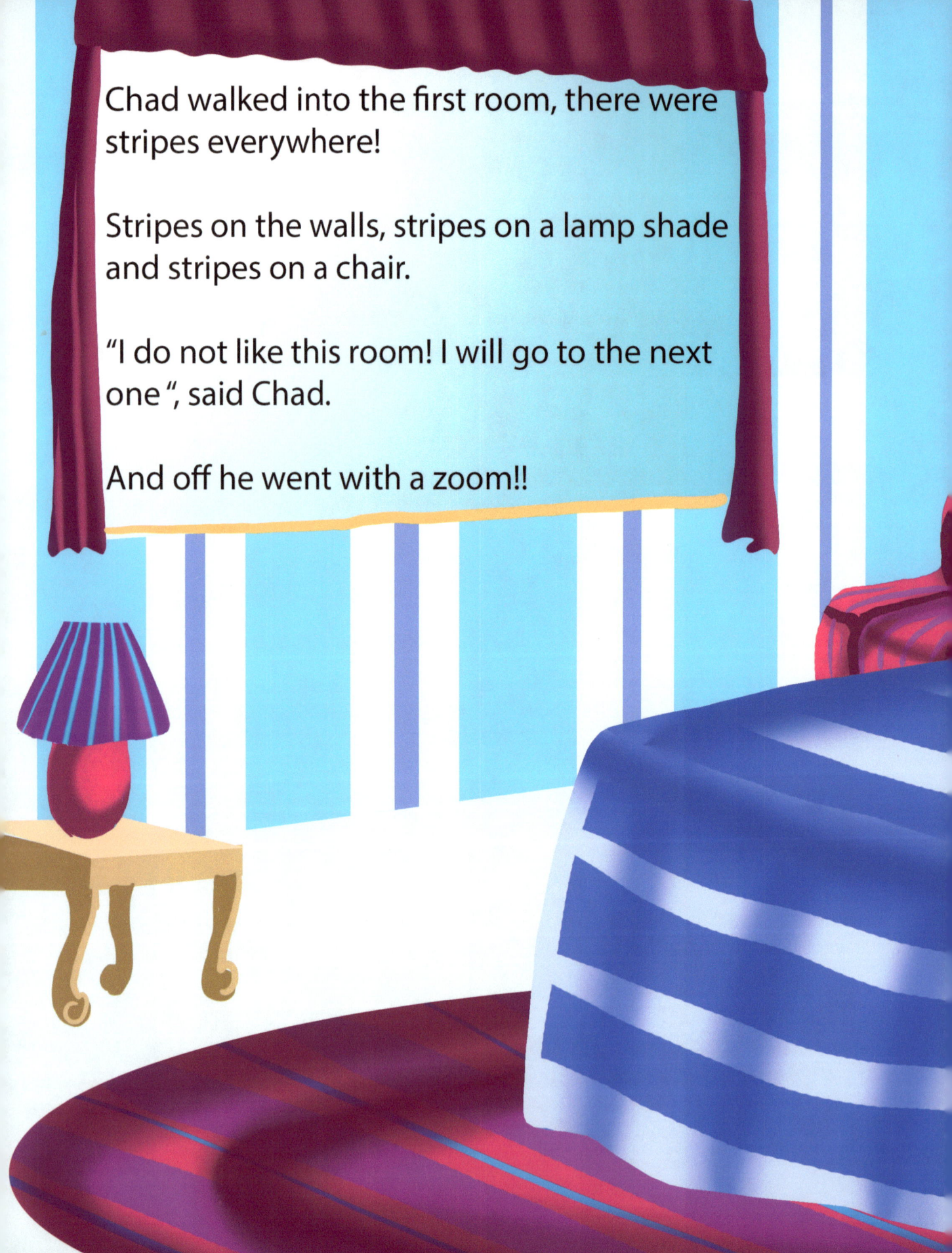

Chad walked into the first room, there were stripes everywhere!

Stripes on the walls, stripes on a lamp shade and stripes on a chair.

"I do not like this room! I will go to the next one ", said Chad.

And off he went with a zoom!!

The second room had POLKA DOTS all around.

This room had dots of green, orange, and blue even on the door, POLKA DOTS could be found.
"I do not like this room! I will go to the next one," said Chad.

And off he went with a zoom!!

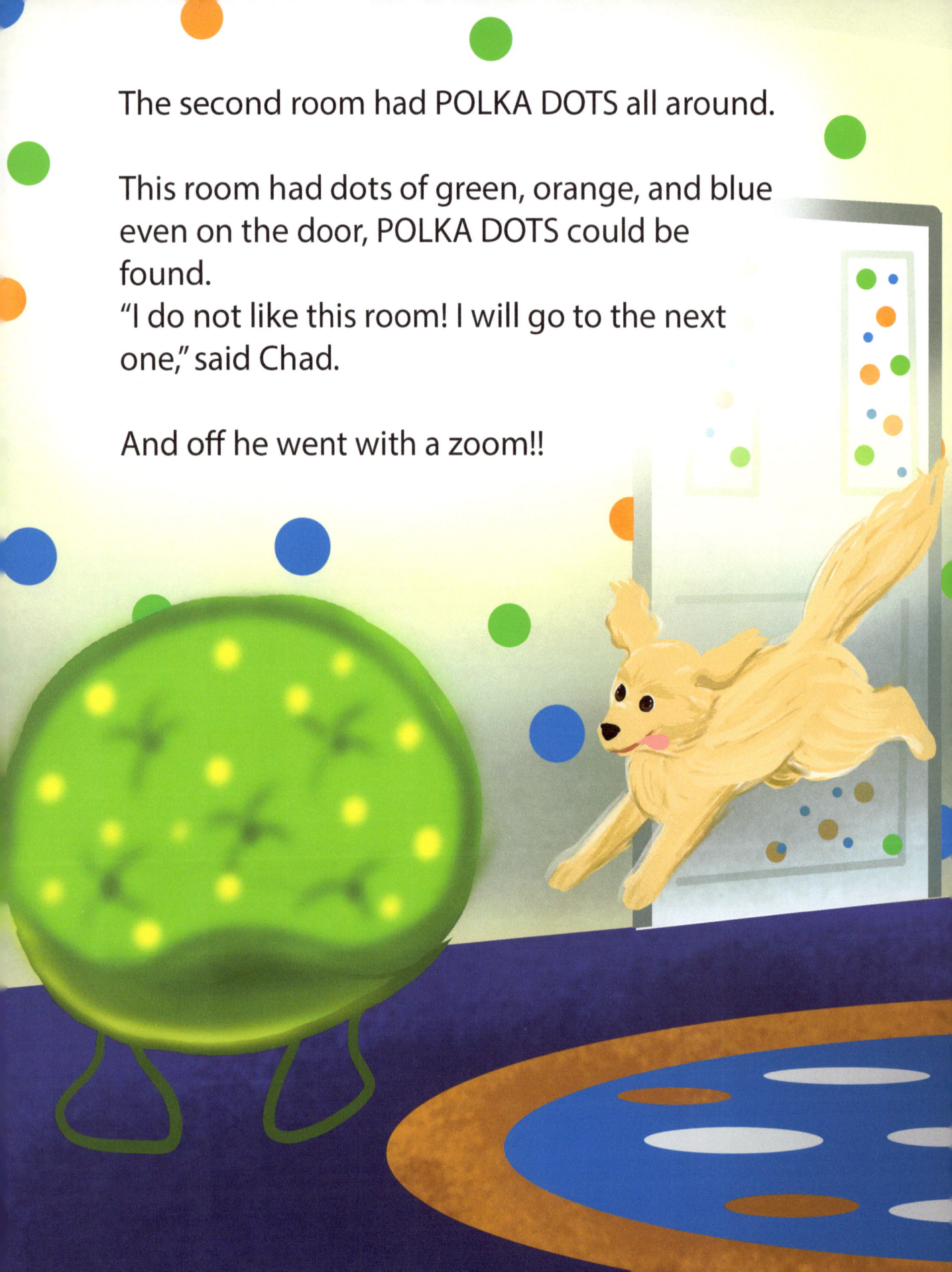

Chad walked into the third room and he could not believe his eyes!

This room had HEARTS on the ceiling and walls.

Which was a big surprise!

"I do not like this room! I will go to the next one," said Chad.

And off he went with a zoom!!

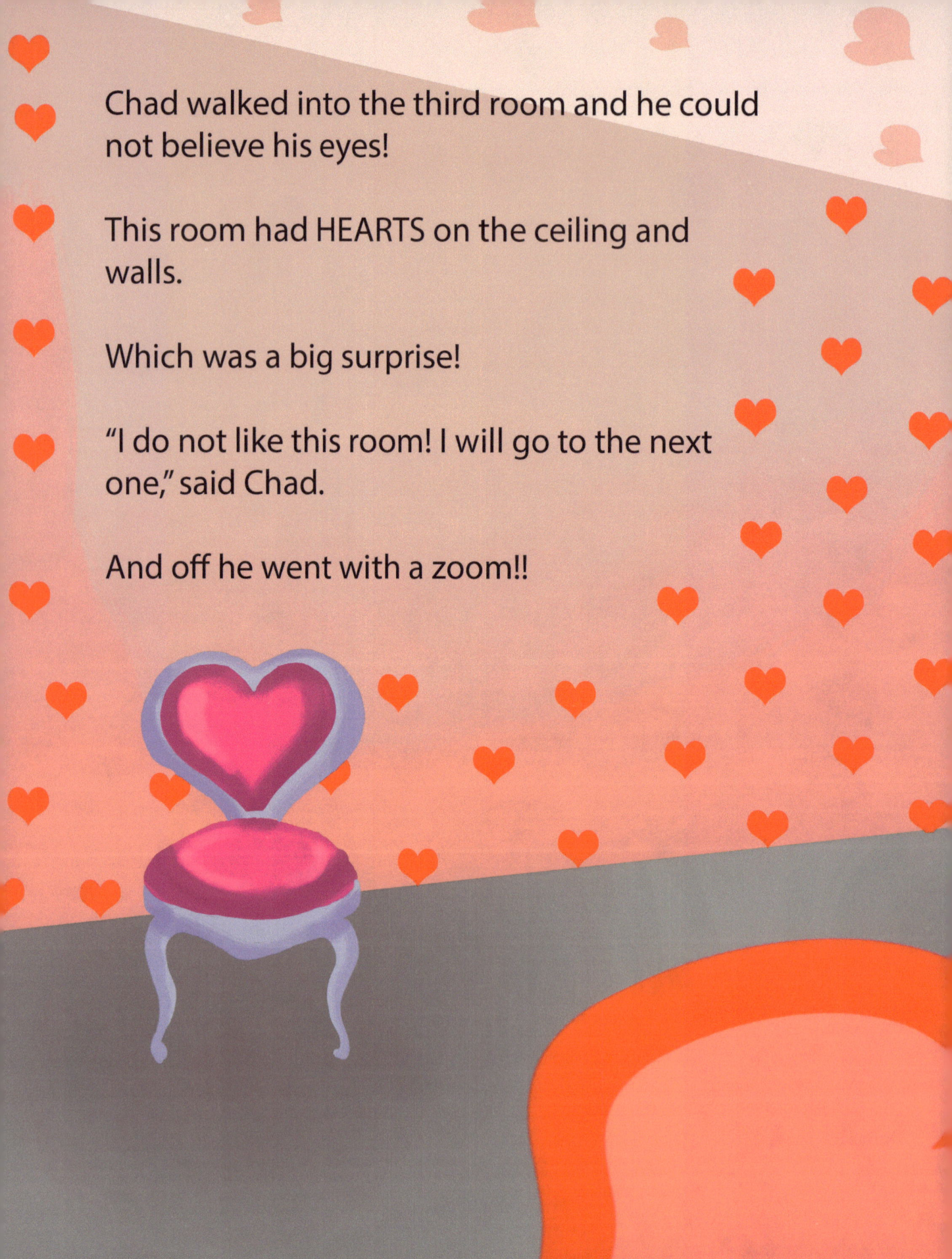

It was the last room for Chad to see, and he took a peep. But when he got to this room, Chad was tired from looking in all the other rooms and fell fast asleep.

The last room was the PLAID room.

Chad was excited when he woke up!

He was happy to see PLAID pillows, PLAID chairs, PLAID sheets, a PLAID cover, and a PLAID cup.

"I found something I can do!" said Chad.

So he took the PLAID pillow and placed it between his paws and began to chew.

The fluff from the pillow was all in the air.

It covered everything including the floor and the plaid chair.

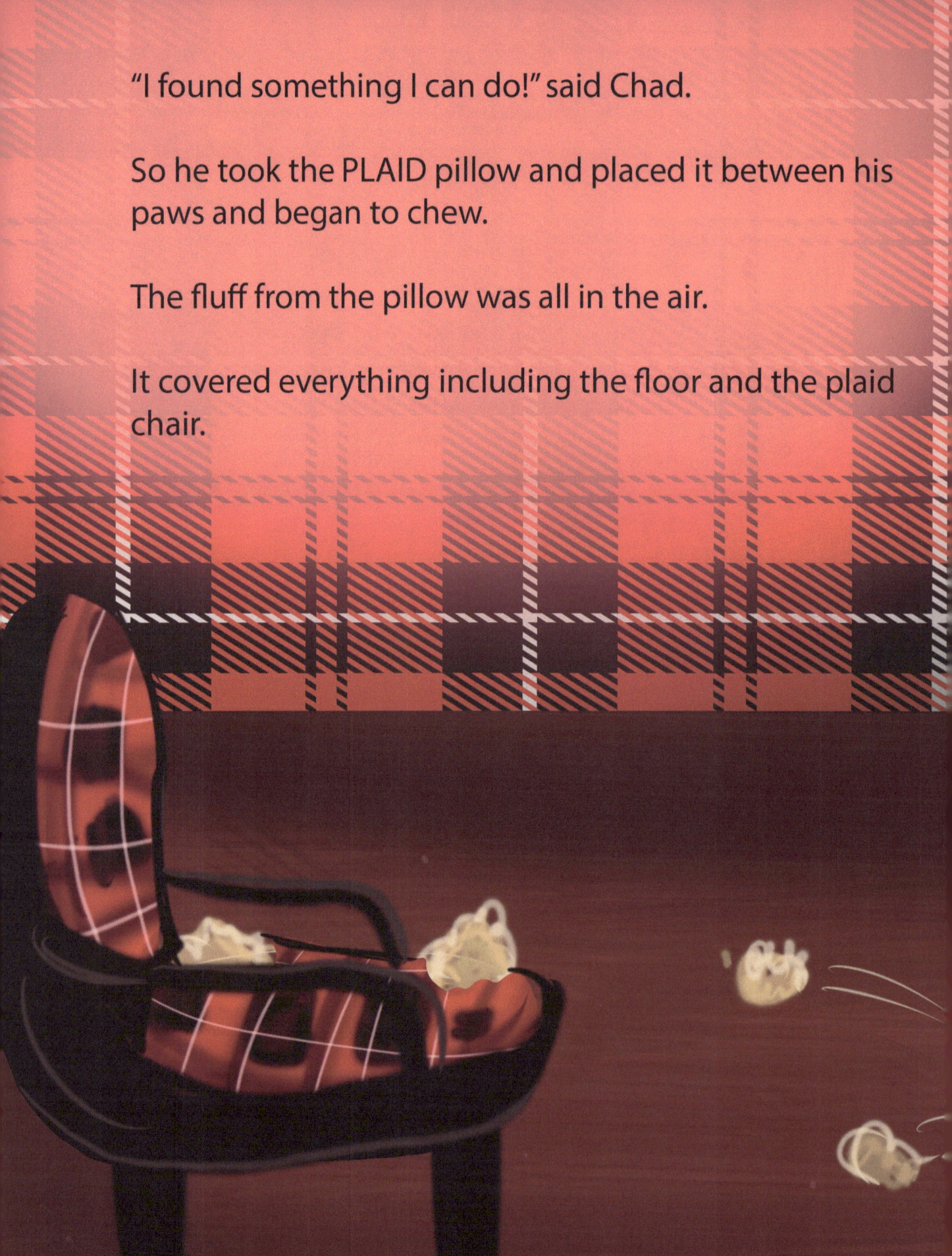

Yo came home, and saw that Brad was sleeping, so she went upstairs to look for Chad.

Chad heard the stairs creeking.

He was scared and hiding under the PLAID sheet, but he did not realize that you could see his cute, little feet.

Yo searched each of the three rooms looking for Chad with a fast heartbeat.

Until she walked into the last room and saw Chad's cute, little feet and small tail wagging under the PLAID sheet.

Yo said to Chad, "I thought you were being bad, but now I see that you really like PLAID.

You are a good boy and I believe you like this room the best!"

"My good boy!
Tomorrow Chad, I will dress you in a PLAID vest!"

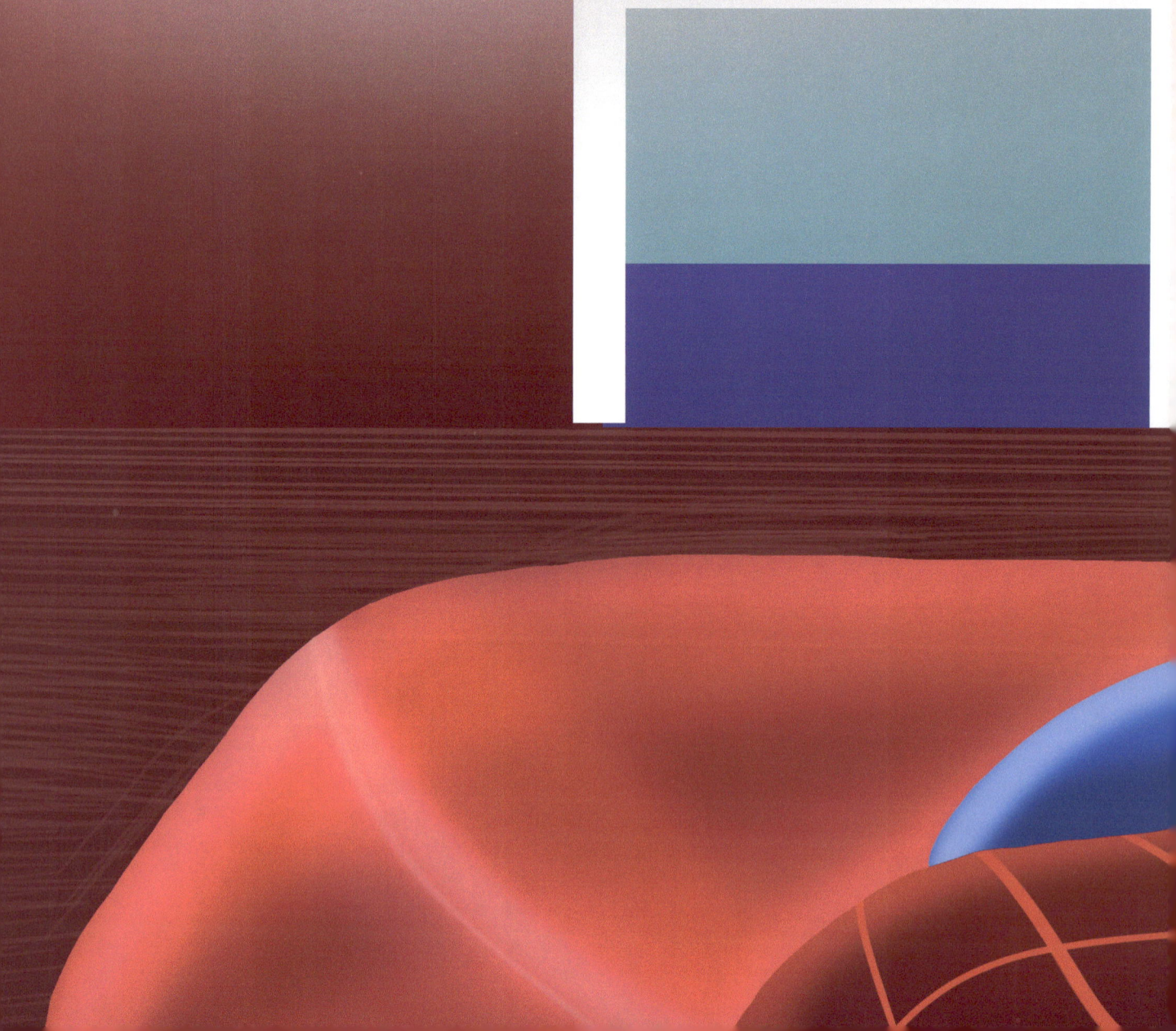

Brad

Yo

Chad

THE END